Worth Giving Up

OMONEFE OISEDEBAMEN ERUOTOR

Redefiners
Nigeria.
redefinersph@gmail.com

Cover design by Yinka Noiki

ISBN: 978-978-981-075-8

DEDICATION

To my aunt, Mrs. Patience Iyamuosa, for exposing me to God early. My life is better because of spiritual strength I have drawn from Him through the different phases of my life.

To Tega, Brume, Tejiri and their children yet unborn, who are growing and will grow in an era different from mine, but need intellectual, spiritual and emotional fortitude to sail through and finish strong.

CONTENTS

Acknowledgments   i

Chapter One   1

Chapter Two   17

Chapter Three   41

Chapter Four   55

Chapter Five   67

Chapter Six   93

Glossary   114

Author's Note   116

About the Author   117

ACKNOWLEDGMENTS

I want to appreciate everyone who has made this book a success; my kids and all the young people I have worked with at one time or another, they inspire me daily to write for young people; Pamela Agboga who did an awesome job with editing; Yinka Noiki for the graphic design; Pastor Tony Aleogena-Raphael for his balanced perspective on spirituality and humanity; Pastors Chris Ubamadu, Wole Ogunnaike, Bisi Ilori and David Takefe, Prof. Odaro Uhumwangho and a host of others through whom I have been mentored at one point or another. Also, I am grateful to my mum (Lucy O. Akhimien) and other family members - Ehisuoria Akhimien, Pauline Omogbelehan and Florence Ijeh-Obiekea – for their support, my friend, Anwuli Ik-Iyoha, and every other person who keeps cheering me on this journey.

Thank you!

Worth Giving Up

CHAPTER ONE

Their second year had just begun. Chito and Lara were no longer Jambitos, as first-year students were tagged. They walked into their first class for the semester and found the lecturer unsurprisingly absent. Most lecturers usually did not show up for their first classes.

The hall had received a shoddy facelift. The blackboard had been replaced with a white one which required markers instead of chalk, but the broken windows and dirty walls were exactly as they had been the semester before. Only a handful of students had arrived and everyone was chatting.

"Chito, let's go back to the hostel," Lara said hurriedly, refusing to go beyond the door.

"Come in, let's say hello to our friends and chat a

bit, then we can leave if the lecturer still hasn't shown up," Chito responded.

"Let's go and get snacks downstairs then come back to check on the class."

Chito wondered what the issue was, but she decided not to probe just then.

"What's up?" she eventually asked as they walked toward the kiosks.

"That guy David is in class," was all Lara said.

The expression of anger on Lara's face upset her friend. "So, because of one guy, you won't go to class?" Chito hissed in mock anger.

"We met back home during the holidays and he asked me out."

"Are you going to run from every guy that asks you out?" Chito queried a shy Lara who merely cast her a warning glance and walked ahead. Chito easily caught up with her, but they changed the subject immediately.

They got drinks and meat pies from the Planet Shop, a small but well-fitted snack shop with air conditioning. The shop also did print jobs and made photocopies, but there were only four chairs for people to sit on. They ate quickly because of the sharp glances the girl at the counter gave them whenever a customer bought snacks and could not get a place to sit down. As they walked back towards the lecture hall, they met David coming down the stairs with his friend Simon.

"No need to go all the way up, he's not coming," was his timely answer to a question they did not ask. Lara quickly muttered an okay that even Chito could not hear and started walking away slowly. David looked at Chito mischievously.

"Can I borrow Lara for a minute?" he asked.

"Of course." Chito laughed within herself because face-offs with guys usually made Lara uncomfortable; she would literally enter the ground. Chito watched her go aside with him, not realising she was giggling quietly until Simon's, "Are you laughing at your friend?" startled her. The laughter that had welled up on her inside came out in a rush. She covered her mouth with one hand, shaking her head defensively. "No, no, no."

Simon responded with a knowing, "Hmm," smiling from ear to ear and raising his brows mockingly. She laughed, this time calmly, and he glanced at her again before looking away.

"Why did you look at me like that?" she asked,

suspicious of his furtive glance.

He looked at her again. "I always thought you were a snob."

"Snob, ke?" exclaimed a bewildered Chito. She was about to say more when Lara touched her from behind.

"Chito, let's go."

She lingered a bit, bade Simon goodbye, and they eventually left. Chito noticed that Lara looked tense and angry as they walked. Clearly, her phobia for men was still there. Chito waited for her to speak about it before she said another word.

"This guy is just disturbing me," she said, looking very upset.

"Just tell him you are in a relationship! Why are you giving yourself a headache for nothing?"

"I don't want it to look like I'm saying no because of another person. I want him to know that it's because I'm a Christian."

"Then just tell him! Instead of making him feel you're playing hard to get," Chito said, laughing at her friend. When she realised her friend was not smiling, she stopped.

Chito knew Lara needed to be straight with David.

However, she also knew that David's advances could cause Lara to reevaluate her current relationship.

~~~~~

The next Saturday, the girls were relaxing in their room when Lara's phone rang. She dropped the nail file she had been working on her nails with and picked the phone from the top of her fridge where it was charging. As she answered the call, Chito lifted her eyes from the book she was reading and listened intently to the conversation her friend was having with her fiancé. Was this all one could get from a godly relationship? Certainly, the world of fiction had painted an exaggerated picture of true love, but were Christians bound to live without the fun part?

She was quick to pry when Lara ended the call because she pitied her for being bound to a choice which was truly not hers, but her pastor's. Though Chito couldn't claim to be knowledgeable enough to draw the line between pastor's choice and hers, she had resolved that she needed more fun than she was witnessing in her friend's relationship.

Lara passed on greetings from Dapo, and Chito said a hesitant "Okay," still trying to take in the conversation
~~~~~

she had just overheard.

"No kisses blown, no 'I love you' said, no 'I miss you'?" she asked, gesticulating with her hands to show her disgust.

Lara was indifferent. "*Abeg jo, which kind kisses?*"

"*The thing no dey shack you?*" Chito asked. It was all she could mutter from the numerous questions on her mind.

Lara, on the other hand, was still wondering why Chito could not let go of the mushy part of love and prepare for the future. "We are already engaged and he is working. All I need do is finish school, then we will have the wedding and move on from there," a resolute Lara defended her self-imposed prison sentence.

It sounded too rigid and dreary for Chito; she wanted more. What an unromantic relationship, she thought. Lara had however made up her mind and trying to change it was difficult. It reminded Chito of her parents. Her dad, a pastor, always treated her mother like a maid. She was a housewife who had never been allowed to get a job. When she eventually started a small business at home that was yielding good profit, he had ordered her to stop.

She was not allowed to sit with him when his

friends were around. Chito had been bemused to see him carry a bag for his friend's wife, saying she had too much luggage on her; something he would never do for his own wife. Chito sighed as she recalled the way he would send her mother to get a toothpick, a napkin, his handkerchief, some water, his Bible and what have you. The worst part was that he was well travelled but Chito's mother had never set foot outside the country. In fact, while she would be grateful if he allowed her to visit her relatives or the friends she didn't have, he happily sponsored his friend's wife to South Africa for a conference the previous year, saying it was to appreciate her good work in church.

The tale of her parents' marriage was one she had narrated to Lara over and over, but Chito was resigned to the fact that if Lara was still bent on marrying her Dapo, there was nothing she could do.

For her part, Chito had made up her mind not to be in the same predicament as her mother. She knew she needed fun. She had known the Lord early, following Him resolutely with a conviction that God was real. Yet, she also decided that she would not marry a man who wouldn't let her walk beside him on the path of life.

~~~~~
~~~~~

Chito was seated in front of a group of girls one evening after the fellowship meeting, waiting for Lara to finish her unit meeting. The girls apparently didn't know she was Lara's friend and she was disappointed when she saw that the sisters' leader was one of them. The group was talking about how Lara didn't really mix with them, and the leader, Stella, said she heard Lara had a boyfriend abroad which could be the source of her pride.

One of the others quickly exclaimed, "No wonder!" as if she just found the answer she sought.

Chito was angry, not because they gossiped about her friend, but because Lara needed help, not a hunt. These girls disdained her for the same reason she needed them. Lara didn't talk much, especially with people she wasn't close to, but Chito felt she needed to talk with someone who was not her home pastor or a member of her home church who believed her destiny was tied to her pastor. It was this belief system that had pushed Lara into a relationship with a guy she barely knew; a guy who could not visit his home country to see his parents or his fiancée. She truly needed other brethren, but there they were, shredding her to pieces like a sheet of toilet paper.

Chito loved her school fellowship. She'd had many

wonderful encounters with God through fellowship there, but the fact that some of the greatest gossips in existence happened to be there hurt really bad. They seemed to be in everyone's business. Some would say that they were praying for God to change a particular person, while others would claim they were speaking about issues so that they wouldn't keep grudges, just like these sisters talking about Lara. But the truth was that they gave information to third parties without bringing them first to the attention of the people in question, when talking to the main party was the proper thing to do.

As Chito walked towards the entrance to say hello to her friend Charles, she witnessed a movie scene first hand, one that made her laugh like someone who just won a lottery, although Charles felt she was being mean. Stella fell down right outside the fellowship venue; one of her heels had given way when she tried to skip a broken stair. Fellowship members ran to her rescue immediately, including Lara who was oblivious of what had been said about her earlier. Chito just had to tell Charles why she had laughed. After listening to her, he reminded her that she was supposed to love everyone. They walked together, and Charles stopped over to greet Stella. Chito walked ahead and waited for him and Lara.

"Chito, that was unfair. Why were you being mean?" a surprised Lara chided her friend for the nonchalant attitude.

"Chito there was no excuse for that," added Charles, making her feel bad about her actions.

"Seriously sha, I am just wondering what I would have done if such a thing happened to me," replied Chito, whispering a quick prayer for forgiveness.

"What if God allowed that sort of thing to happen to me whenever I sin?" she thought, humbled.

~~~~~

One cool Friday evening, as the two friends walked back from an evening lecture, they noticed that the car park was packed full. A multi-national company was having a talent show.

"Not again," exclaimed Lara who was sick and tired of the constant noise that exuded from such activities. "Hey Lara, there will definitely be free drinks. And see, souvenirs are being passed around. But I'm too tired. At least the rooms will be less noisy than usual," added Chito who was glad that she could sleep peacefully, as she was certain that
~~~~~

all their roommates would be at the gig. "Let's buy food at the common room," suggested Lara, leading her friend towards the shops at the common room where they could purchase prepacked meals and snacks. They walked to the food kiosk but the lady was nowhere to be found. Apparently, she had gone to the gig as well and left her wares.

"This woman is totally unserious. How could she leave all these things unattended just because of one fake show?" said Chito.

"To you it is fake, but to her, it means the world," an irritated Lara replied.

"See all the other students who have come and gone, do you know how much she has lost in this short time? Let's just buy snacks."

"Snacks alone are dry, and I don't want to take sugar again today,"

"Hmmm, weight watcher, you better eat," Chito advised.

"Is it your body?" Lara asked rhetorically.

"Oh, really? And I'm the one who measures your arm circumference every week. You will start doing that on your own."

"Okay, sorry na?" pleaded a repentant Lara who knew she needed her friend's help.

"Only if you pay for dinner."

"Is it not a joke? Why should I buy you snacks?"

"Deal or no deal?" asked Chito smiling from ear to ear.

"Okay, deal Chito, but I will get you big time."

"Try me", she said walking straight to the kiosk and scanning through the items displayed for her pick. "These snacks are stale," she announced.

"We don't have an option" responded Lara, "Let's make do with the stale snacks and go to bed."

Other students came to the food kiosk and left when there was no one to sell to them. Chito and Lara paid for their dinner and had to leave their change because they went with the bottles which they would return the next day in exchange for their change.

As they walked back, past the empty TV room, the electricity went out and they could hear the screams from different corners of the hostel and a loud and harmonious, '*Okpari!*' from the crowd at the car park, a traditional slang used when situations were terrible.

They found their way into the room and switched

on Chito's rechargeable lamp which was as bright as regular electric bulbs. The room was really quiet, and since they both shared a tiny corner with a six-spring bed, having an empty room meant one person could sleep in another roommate's bed until the owner returned.

"Thank God there is no one else in this room," Chito pointed out as she fell with a thud, landing on her back on Precious' bed.

"Yes oh! Our six-spring bed will not carry excess luggage today," replied Lara, and they both laughed as the lights came back on.

"Up Nepa!" Their shouts joined the chorus from students all over the campus, as if they were all singing to a particular rhythm, rejoicing that the electric authority had restored power.

"Why am I even lying on Precious' bed? She complained the last time that I did not make it properly," said Chito, as she slowly got up from the bed and began straightening out the sheets.

"That girl is weird," added Lara. "I wonder how she copes elsewhere. Don't touch my this, don't touch my that," dramatising as she spoke. "Haba! She cannot even lie on the same bed with someone. Last week, her sister returned a shirt she borrowed from her, washed. Her comment was that it had been worn by her sister so she had to wash it again, even though the girl had washed it before returning. Her sister, not a stranger oh." She snapped the fingers on both hands and raised her shoulders simultaneously to show her disdain.

"Is that not how you are?" Chito added jokingly to her friend who refuted the accusation immediately with, "God forbid," a phrase that was in harmony with a knock on their door.

Lara went for the door while Chito sat on their bed, peeping to see who it was. It was John, a mutual friend who never knew the right time to visit. Chito frowned but tried to be accommodating. So, both girls who had made ready for bed had to receive a guest.

"Hello Lara," John said. John needed help with an assignment as he had been away from school for a while due to illness. "Please, can I borrow your 221 textbook?"

She rummaged in her wardrobe and gave it to him, unhappy but refusing to show it. "How far have you gone?" she asked, showing some genuine concern.

"I am still trying to understand Statistics. I was not there when the lecturer started the topic, so it is a bit difficult to understand."

Lara and Chito tried to explain from their own reservoir of knowledge, but John was still not able to grasp the finer points.

"Can I keep your book till tomorrow?" he asked Lara who willingly let him go with it, partly because he needed it and partly because she wanted him to leave as soon as possible.

John gratefully bade goodbye, but the girls were not happy with the hour and a half sleep time they had lost.

"We can't continue like this" suggested Chito as she straightened the bed. "We need to get accommodation off-campus."

Lara burst into laughter immediately. "The last time I mentioned getting off-camp accommodation, you said it was because I was anti-social. Now, you are mixing with the whole world, please stay here."

Chito eyed her and hissed jokingly. "I will walk around all the quarters in this school till I get off-camp accommodation. You can't even sleep or eat without someone barging in on you, mtchew," she hissed again. The fatigue showed in her eyes as she changed into her nightie and wiped her face with baby wipes, before lying on her bed for the night.

"I don't like the noise either and that was why I fought for it initially, but I also don't want to be isolated off-camp. It is difficult to get transportation out of those locations," Lara said as she climbed up to Sasha's bed. The first-year student's bunk was right above theirs. "Well, let's just try and see, we need to read more in our last two years," she concluded.

They gave their subject matter some more thought until they dropped off to sleep, but the show in the car park stayed on till way past midnight.

CHAPTER TWO

The second semester ended. Like most students, and based on their decision during the last academic year; the most important thing for Lara and Chito was getting accommodation off-campus so they could be more comfortable and enjoy some privacy in their third year, rather than being in the hostels where the overcrowded rooms were open to all. Chito was more agile in the search and even when Lara was not available, she went about it alone, hopeful for a catch. She had gone from house to house at the Doctors' Quarters, searching for a spare room in their boys' quarters, but found none.

"Will you wait till I'm back from home?" asked a concerned Lara, she knew her friend was eager.

"That would be Monday," replied Chito who did

not want to waste any day because thousands of students were also searching and Lara was going home for the weekend on a Friday, to return on Sunday evening.

"If we still don't get at the staff quarters, can we get outside the school premises?"

"Noooo, my father will just ask me to come back home," wailed Chito who lived twenty minutes from the school gate.

"That's true! I didn't think of that fact," said Lara whose family lived a bit far from the school premises, though her dad worked at the school.

That Saturday evening, Chito decided to go round some houses she had visited previously but had not met the occupants. She went from house to house, knocking and talking, making a friend or two. Just as she left the last house on Road A, it started to rain. She ran into the Senior Staff Club which was close by to take shelter, as she had not taken an umbrella along. She was greeted at the gate by the smell of burning cigarettes combined with the sweet smell of suya; grilled meat with traditional spices. The latter was tempting but the money she had left would not buy a reasonable quantity as she had spent almost all that she had taken for the day moving from place to place on her quest. So, she just walked up to the bar and got a bottle of Fanta.

On the right, some guys were playing snooker and there was such loud music that she had to strain her ears to hear the newsflash on the LCD TV that hung on the wall. There seemed to be a few lecturers in the inner lounge playing chess. She wondered if their kids were the ones dancing drunk very close to the snooker board. Chito took her drink quietly, like a fish out of water, looking around to find a familiar face, and truly, she did find one. Simon, David's friend. His glance met hers as he paid off the suya man and ran quickly from the suya shed to the outdoor bar where she was.

"What are you doing here?" he asked, pleasantly surprised.

"I am looking for accommodation," she replied sadly, "and the rain got me stuck here, so I'll leave when it stops."

He pulled up a stool and sat next to her.

"Won't you go back, your suya will get cold?" she said, but he just looked at her and laughed.

"Why are you laughing?" she asked wondering

what he found amusing.

"You are taking a cold drink and shivering," he said, amazed at her choice.

"Oh," she exclaimed, laughing at herself as well. "It was the only thing I could get while waiting for the rain to subside." She laughed again, and he still looked at her pitifully, but she wanted to finish her drink.

Surprisingly, he unwrapped his suya and asked her to join him. Initially, she turned him down politely, but when he tried to feed her, she knew she had to do it herself. The hot delicacy was a great relief to her quivering body, and the taste was superb. The pepper, on the other hand, was not friendly, as she was coughing in no time after a little pepper had gone through her nasal cavity. She took a sip of her drink and ran towards the gate. The rain had gone down and she felt funny coughing out there. Simon went with her, bringing along the wrap of suya; and when she was okay, he walked her back to the bar where they took their positions on their stools again and Chito finished her drink in one long gulp.

"Wait! What did you just do?" Simon shouted, trying to drag the bottle from her.

"What are you doing?" she queried. He looked at her and looked away, then glanced her way a couple more times.

"You are acting strange," she said to him because she didn't understand his glances.

So he explained to her that going back to drinks left previously was not safe in that environment, because he had heard a lot of times of people putting sleeping pills into them.

"Do you live close by," she asked.

He nodded in affirmation, pointing to the house opposite the club gate. "I live there," he said, smiling. "David and I are roommates."

"How do you cope with all this noise?" she asked, looking at him with eyes full of pity.

"It is not very noisy at the boys' quarters since it is behind the main house." He didn't stop smiling. She was uneasy and quickly took advantage of the fact that the rain had subsided to gather her things to leave.

"Why not stay a little longer, so you won't be wet, it is still drizzling." It was really drizzling and he did sometimes catch a cold from drizzles.

"I'll walk you", he said to her when he noticed her resolution. He walked her out of the club, still glancing at her occasionally.

"Simon, I'm fine" she eventually said in response to his stolen glances.

"Don't mind me," was his response, "I feel responsible for not warning you ahead, but thank God you are okay."

"I'm a big girl" she replied, "I can take care of myself."

He just smiled, putting both hands in his pockets with the suya nylon dangling out of the right, walking beside her.

The evening was a bit chilly and the pine trees which lined the streets swayed in rhythm to the music of the wind. The identical houses were always a joy to behold for Chito and though she was a bit uncomfortable walking with Simon who she did not know very well, she appreciated the beauty around her which was a sharp contrast to the students' halls of residence.

She wanted to complete the trip to the bus park alone, but Simon was adamant about being her chaperone.

She felt lucky as they passed by the last house before the turn to the park because someone called Simon from the other side of the road and he told the guy he would be with him shortly. She thought he would leave but he tried to buy some time, asking her to relax.

"The park is just over there," she said, she could see the park from where she stood and so could he.

"I just need to give him something from my room, please wait here," he said, pulling her in front of a house which had its outdoor security lights turned on. Obviously, she knew he wanted to be able to see her from where he was or to make sure she wasn't in the dark and quiet street alone. But she couldn't wait there looking around aimlessly, so she decided to head for the park before he returned. She could see a bus and hear the conductor calling passengers for Hall One and decided to make a run for it.

As she ran, she felt like something was thumping in her head and somehow slowing her senses. Still, she tried to keep the pace so she could go to the lit part of the street, but she stumbled and fell. "Jesus" she whispered, confused. She felt unfortunate because she had crossed to the dark part where no one could see her; but then it happened suddenly, deterioration beyond explanation. A scream for help bubbled up in her head but didn't get to her lips. She tried to lift a hand but it fell limp by her side; so she prayed to God in her heart because it was clear that he alone could save her.

Just then, two boys walked her way; they looked drunk and she recognised one of them from the bar. She was glad that help had come, drunk or not, and tried to move again, but blacked out. She woke up dreamily when she felt her shirt go off. She didn't understand and couldn't get up but she heard raised voices and felt someone lift her, then she went blank again.

~~~~~

It was a long night, Chito's dreams were many, scary and short. She rolled over and over on the bed, her head was pounding and she could not get up. She had forgotten all that happened at the Doctors' Quarters; her dreams had stolen her memory. Eventually, she woke up, felt for her bedside table but was surprised to touch empty space. Her eyes shot open and she tried to get up but did so with difficulty. Simon came to her rescue. He sat her up but
~~~~~

she could not keep still so he sat behind her and placed his hand on her shoulder to keep her steady.

"What's going on?" she asked him, scared of the worst.

"Just relax Chito, you are fine," he said hoping to reassure her but filling her to the brim with fear instead.

"Relax? How?" She struggled to get off the bed because even though he tried to calm her, her inability to explain her own situation made it difficult to stay calm. As the rusty ceiling fan went about its dance – around ritual, her heart beat faster. She put her feet down in a bid to stand, but they could not hold her weight so she stumbled, but Simon's arms were there, he raised her up and held her steady.

"Chito you are not strong enough for this, just chill," Simon said reassuringly, helping her back to bed and sitting behind her in support, the way he had done earlier?

"I can't just 'chill', what is going on?" she asked, kicking her feet in the air, somewhat uneasy because her blouse was off, she was just wearing a tube top, and her bra straps were visible to him. "What happened?" she asked again, expecting the worst. So this time, she did not look at him but at the door, just glancing at him once in a while until he spoke.

He looked at her intently, and his voice sounded hoarse as he said, "Some guys tried to rape you."

"What!" she screamed, trying to recall anything she could. She felt like she was being sawn in two with her eyes wide open. She cried uncontrollably and Simon held her really close. "Are you sure they didn't do it?" she asked, hoping he was not just trying to make her feel good. She was quivering like a child but dried her tears as they poured.

"I came back with my friend Desmond and did not meet you where I left you, so I trailed you on the path to the bus park when I saw two guys trying to take your shirt off; Desmond and I warded them off, and I tried to rescue you while he ran after them, but they got away. I took you to my BQ first of all, but my landlord who saw us carry you in, insisted that we took you to the Health Centre, and I am glad we did.

Before she could take it all in, the door flung open and Lara ran in with David behind her. Obviously, Simon had told David and he had gone to get Lara. The girls hugged and wiped tears. Lara started bringing clothes out for her friend when the doctor walked in.

"Good morning, sir" she greeted and he smiled. Her friends also smiled but she didn't understand why, until the doctor said: "It is evening."

"How is that possible?" She asked wondering just how long she had slept and the doctor went on to explain, "You were given a form of sedative which we suspect was put in your drink. It made you sleep, but don't worry you'll be okay now." He added jokingly that she had been talking in her sleep about how Simon had warned her.

She cast a glance at Simon, remembering what he had said, but the deed was done. The doctor asked Simon to move and Chito to raise her head, then he propped her up with a pillow for a proper examination.

"What can I do now?" She asked the doctor who was looking into her eyes with a tiny torch. "All you need is rest, you'll be fine, we flushed the drug out of your system, and you'll regain strength with time," he said reassuringly.

"Doctor, are you sure they did not do it?" She asked wondering how he knew she was not raped.

"We checked you," the doctor replied, understanding her fear, "and I'm sure they did not." He reminded her that her friends would be with her.

Her mind couldn't help but imagine what they must have done while checking her, the mere thought sent cold chills down her spine. In a bid to reassure her, the doctor informed her that they had called her parents, but she froze like an Egyptian mummy.

"How did you get their number?"

He laughed and said her mobile phone had come in handy. It was funny, she laughed too but was scared. When the doctor left, tears dropped from her eyes and Simon asked her why she was crying, but she could not answer. He went back to her side; pulling his chair close, he sat by her while the others tried to say words of encouragement.

"Lara you know Popsie, now? Chito asked her friend rhetorically, this time Lara placed her right hand on Chito's shoulder, wiping her own tears with the other. David tried to place his hands on Lara's shoulder but she shrugged him off. Just then, Chito's phone rang. Her mother cried as she asked if she was okay. Chito responded tearfully with words that reassured the woman that she had not been raped.

"Thank you, Jesus," her mother repeated over and over, grateful for her daughter's life.

But when her dad took the phone, the tone changed. "How could you have been so careless?" he screamed into the receiver. "Don't you have common sense? Are you supposed to walk alone in the dark? You better thank God they failed, what kind of embarrassment would you have brought to this family if you got pregnant?" He sighed and cut the line.

She cried as she put her phone down. How could he still speak like that at such a time? She just cried and Lara tried to be there for her, as she had always done, while Simon held her hand.

"Let me feed you, Chito," Simon offered the food he had bought.

"Don't worry," she said shyly. "Thanks, but let Lara do it."

"Sorry Chito, I need to see my dad, I left a textbook at home and he has promised to meet me at the main gate shortly to return it."

Chito released Lara and was left with Simon and David, angry though that the doctor had to fix the drip on her right hand, because on the left it had gone into a tissue, making the hand swell. She could not feed herself or even wave her hand.

A thin nurse walked in with her medication and Chito smiled because though she was seeing her for the first time, she knew her. Students always talked about her; she was a six-footer, surprisingly tall for a nurse. Students called her, 'Yellow Agbani'.

"Has she eaten?" asked Yellow Agbani and when Simon responded in the negative, she asked her to eat immediately. Simon wasted no time after her exit. He went straight to Chito with the bowl, opening it and shoving a spoonful into her mouth. She was forced to accept his care, he fed her until she said she was full, then he picked up the piece of turkey with his fingers and she took a bite out of it.

"I'm okay", she said after three bites, terrified at the thought of her lips touching his fingers. "Thanks."

As he placed the rest back in the bowl and into the bag, she longed for some more but was too shy to ask. She chose to swallow some saliva in place of the well-spiced piece of turkey. He stayed on until the nurse came for her evening injection, they took their leave then and promised to return the next day.

"Thanks for everything," Chito said heartily to Simon and David, grateful that she had been saved. Simon blushed like a lady as he made to leave, but came back to give Chito a reassuring hug. Chito spent the night wondering what would have happened if he had not saved her, he had become her new hero.

As Simon and David walked out of the hospital, Simon placed his hands on his head.

"What's going on in your head?" asked David.

"David, I love this girl," he said looking like a child that has just been caught with a piece of meat.

"A-ah, *slow down now, no be me first chike* her friend? Lara *never gree for me, you wan chike Chito?"* he asked his friend, insinuating that Simon was about to take the lead in a race that he had started.

"Life waits for no man," was Simon's response and they both laughed.

"You know she is a fellowship girl, how will you cope?" was David's next question.

"How are you coping?" Simon retorted jokingly. "I like her sha, she's fun" was his concluding response to his friend's question, and they walked back to their room, discussing their relationship issues.

~~~~~

She was okay when she woke up the next morning, but it was Lara by her bedside. She had hoped to see Simon.

"The doctor says you can leave today," said a delighted Lara who had begun packing her things.

"Praise God," added Chito, relieved to leave the prison cell called hospital and go about her normal business; but there was a tiny tinge of fear in her heart. The doctor came in after a nurse had checked her vital signs; he reviewed her file and wrote in it, then asked how she felt. He looked relieved when he checked the test results brought in that morning by a haughty looking orderly whose trousers seemed to have been worn for the past month without washing.

She hoped Simon would stop by but did not mention it to Lara while they waited for her drugs. Chito was packed and good to go when Yellow Agbani stepped in again. As usual, she was full of smiles.

"Take care of yourself and rest well," she said as
~~~~~

she discontinued the drip and removed the syringes and drugs which were in the room for emergency treatment. "Take your tablets in the morning and evening."

Chito said, "Okay," and thanked her, then without thinking blurted out to her friend, "Where is Simon?" Lara stopped to look at her and she regretted her action immediately, wishing she could take the words back.

"Be careful with that guy!" Lara, obviously, had noticed their growing fondness.

"But I told you what happened," Chito defended, trying to hide the obvious.

"Chito, don't give him false hope," she pleaded. "Remember you are a believer, don't get yourself unequally yoked."

Although Chito knew the truth, she didn't know what to do with the feelings that were growing within her because he was extraordinarily nice to her, and she respected him because he had an opportunity to take advantage of her when she was passed out but he had not. She saw that as a sign of nobility and honesty, traits that were rare in their day.

As they walked out of the centre to get a cab, they ran into Simon who was on his way in. He opted to go back with them to the hostel and Chito was glad. As they walked towards the car park of the Health Centre, they could see other patients. That was the first time Chito had visited the centre, but Lara had done so several times because that was where her family members had access to healthcare.

There was only one taxi in the car park, and though they all wished for a better pick, they had to make do with what was available.

One look at the interior of the taxi made Simon say, "Hope this taxi will not tear my shirt?"

Lara was irritated but decided not to show it, while Chito laughed at him.

"Oga, wetin dey happen?" Simon asked the driver, whose cab had taken a vow of sluggishness, as the ride back to the hostel seemed endless.

"I thought I was the only one wondering," added Chito. She just longed to be back in her room. The old man smiled and kept driving without complaint. He knew his car was not in good condition, but he had to make money. Simon who was in the front seat wondered if the man would not dislocate his wrist, trying so hard to change the stiff gears.

They got to the hostel at about 4:00 pm and Simon, trying to act like a gentleman, helped pull the bags out of the boot and they walked to the gate together before realisation dawned on them.

"Oh! It's not yet time," exclaimed Chito realising that it was not yet time for males to enter the girls' hostel.

"No qualms," said Simon as he gently dropped the bags and Lara picked them up. "Let's go for ice-cream" he offered.

One look at Lara told Chito she was not interested, but the thought of being in the dull room on a day like that made Chito say yes. From the porter's lodge, she could tell that there was no electricity so she did not regret her choice. While Simon waited for her in the common room watching television, she took a quick bath to wash off the hospital sediments, changed her clothes and returned. She was excited and wanted to look good.

Simon gasped, "Wow!" when she walked back into the common room. She was wearing a pair of black Jeans and a V-necked grey t-shirt that complemented her dark skin tone perfectly. She blushed when he moved to her side and took her hand. She was still uncomfortable but didn't protest as they walked out of the hostel towards the ice-cream shop.

The Flavour Shop was well lit. It was relieving to walk from darkness into light, but the noise from the generator made it difficult to hear the movie showing on the 20-inch television screen positioned in a little corner by the door. The establishment made good use of the space they had. Chito received her vanilla ice-cream with joy.

"I wonder why people take chocolate ice-cream," she said, mocking Simon playfully. "To me, frozen chocolate ice-cream tastes like chalk," she continued to a bewildered Simon.

"Have you tasted chalk before?" He asked playfully and was surprised when she nodded in affirmation.

"What!" he screamed, "Why would you eat chalk?" he queried.

"In primary school, a lot of us tasted chalk. Didn't you?"

He shook his head. "What else do you eat that I need to know about? Tell me now before I take you home and you start eating up strange stuff." They laughed and his remark caught her attention, but she chose to shake it off.

"There's nothing between us," she thought, deceiving herself. As she took another spoonful of ice-cream, a guy ran past wearing a grey shirt, just like one of the guys in her memory who had tried to hurt her. She froze like the cream itself. The memory of being drugged suddenly became real. In a flash, thoughts of the possibility of a second experience swept through her mind and she became scared.

Simon told her she would be okay. He sensed what was wrong and encouraged her to take the ice-cream, assuring her it wasn't drugged. She became a bit melancholy but encouraged herself. As she resumed taking her ice-cream, he glanced at her occasionally as if he wanted to say something, but it reminded her of the way he glanced at her the day she was drugged.

"Why are you looking at me like that?" she asked uneasily.

"You're just licking the ice-cream," he pointed out, his thin lips spread out in an unusual smile. "What will you use to eat your cone?"

It was not an issue for her; she wondered why it was for him.

Chito grew shaky as the day darkened. She knew she was not in a secluded environment like the day at the Doctors' Quarters, but she was uncomfortable. Even if she didn't expect it to happen again, she found herself imagining what she would do if she were ever attacked. She told Simon she wanted to go back to rest, but she was running from her thoughts and he willingly walked her back.

"The evening is really cool, it seems like it's going to rain," observed Chito while Simon looked up to see the sky for his own reading. "Thanks again for everything," she said, meaning every word.

He squeezed her shoulder. "Anytime."

They walked slowly to the girls' hostel, talking about their preparations for the exams which were fast approaching and how he would help her catch up with academic work. At the hostel entrance, they lingered a bit, concluding their discussion.

"I would have loved to come in with you Chito, but I think you need more rest than a chat."

"Same here Simon, but I need to sleep," she confirmed, "I am really sleepy."

He gave her a goodnight hug that ushered millions

of butterflies upward from the pit of her stomach, and as he withdrew, he planted a kiss on her forehead whispering, "Goodnight," in the deepest baritone she had ever heard. In his eyes, she saw emotions. His hug made her feel a warmth she had never experienced before. There and then, a bond was established between them, one they were yet to define. She said goodbye as though hypnotised, missing a step or two as she walked to her room because her heart was in chaos.

As she stepped into her corner, she sat on the bed, unable to say a word, but grateful to God that Lara was asleep. She wasn't sure she would have been able to answer her questions if she saw her in that hypnotic state. She took her medication and slipped into her nightwear, too cold for a bath. She spent the time thinking of what to do about her experience with Simon. Thinking of a way to ensure that her dream of waiting until marriage before sex, which had been crested on her heart, came true.

"What about kisses?" Chito said out loud. 'Not even real ones, just forehead kisses?' She wondered who she could ask that wouldn't judge her. Lara was out of the question, someone who couldn't even say *I love you* to her fiancé.

She dreamt of Simon all night, in one dream he was walking her down the aisle and in another, he was leading her to a gang of thieves. The latter was scary, it felt real. She had to remind herself that it was just a dream.

"What are you thinking of?" asked Lara, jolting her out of her line of thought.

"Nothing," she lied.

Lara looked at her, puzzled. "Nothing? Are you okay?"

Chito simply nodded, cringing inside with guilt for lying, a thing she never did.

"Maybe you should rest some more," Lara suggested, worried that the trauma was beginning to take effect on her friend.

"I will," replied Chito, still feeling guilty. Lara who had just woken up took her toiletries on her way out for a bath. Chito guessed she had her suspicions but they both said nothing.

CHAPTER THREE

Mrs Rita Chiazor had had it. She was sitting on her bed at 9:00 am when she would normally have rushed to ensure breakfast was ready for her husband before he went off to church. But the nonchalance he had shown since the day they got the call from the hospital had shot a bolt of resistance into her. This had to stop, she thought. Looking at her image in the dressing mirror close to her bed, she began to cry.

"When did I become this person?" she blurted out.

She looked at herself as she stood up from the bed and fell back amidst tears, as she remembered the incident.

"Thank you Lord for saving my baby," she repeated over and over; pouring out the river of pain that she had held back over the years, the pain of regret, of the loss of herself and the life she had thought she could have. There she was posing as the wife of a pastor who was a saint to the world and a monster in his own bedroom.

"What have I become?" she blurted out again to the God who made her, the one she had given her heart to at age ten and hoped to follow all her life.

"Is this all there is to life?" she thought as she scanned through her life in the twinkle of an eye.

As she sat back up and wiped her eyes, her husband walked into the room holding his briefcase. She had vowed not to be rude but also not to keep putting herself in the line of fire, trying to explain her every move to a man who had told himself he had the devil for a wife.

"So why are you still crying?" shouted an indifferent Rev. Nonso Chiazor. "Is that why my food is not on the table?"

Her eyes shot up in disbelief. She wanted to respond but held her tongue, asking God for the grace to keep it so.

"I hope you will not go to her school against my instruction, because I don't understand these crocodile tears. A girl who was careless enough—"

"A girl who was preserved by the grace of God, by his mercy," she cut in with a low but firm tone in a fit of anger that she had learnt to keep under. "Whether she was careless or not, my only child was preserved and I am glad. But I will be honest with you, Nonso, I do not believe that refusing to see her will please God. So I will go to my child and hear her out, then I will reassure her that everything will be alright and give her good advice on how to ensure this does not happen again."

At that, she walked away hurriedly towards the bathroom door to get ready for a bath, her heart pounding with fear for what would ensue.

"Do you realise that I am the head of this house and you need to obey me?" He was a bit shaken because she had never refused him anything. He was used to having an obedient servant, one who was ready to say yes to his every word.

Instead of returning to his leash willingly, she turned, looked straight into his eyes and said, "My dear husband, before I became a wife, I was a child of God and I must please him first, then you."

"Who said you should not please God?" said Rev. Nonso mockingly.

"I owe it to God to lead my child on the right path and I will please him by doing just that."

Her husband broke into a fit of laughter. She was shocked but went into the bathroom and started brushing her teeth. She was resolute.

Rev. Nonso was angry. He could not understand why his wife would willingly disobey the scripture that said women should submit to their own husbands. "I am off to church," he said to threaten her because that meant he would not ask the driver to come back for her. He waited patiently for her to apologise or plead so he could consider changing his mind.

"I'll see you in church," shouted Mrs Chiazor from the bathroom to a stunned husband who walked away planning his next strategy to teach his wife a lesson.

~~~~~

As the days went by, Chito had to hide her head in shame, as students had spread the news that she had been raped. Some people would look at her pitifully as they said
~~~~~

sorry, never mentioning the suspicions they had. Others would pull her aside and tell her to quickly take abortion pills to help cleanse her system. Her defense that she had not been raped was always met with a pitying, "I understand." They believed she was covering the truth because it felt awkward.

She cried a lot. She wondered why she had taken that gulp. That last single gulp had cost her a lot, too much to bear. Her body still ached from the fall, and maybe the pressure of the guys trying to restrain her. She usually felt some pain a short while before her next dose of medicine because the strength of the dose taken earlier would have gradually started wearing off. She also found it hard to be alone with any guy, except Simon.

Her first day back in fellowship was refreshing, Pastor Chandler's message talked about the mercy of God, explaining how God fought countless battles for people that they did not know about. She was glad she knew one of such battles, God had protected her and ensured that she got help immediately. The reassuring hugs and pats from members after the service gave her hope and strength. They made her feel the love of Jesus as if He was tangibly present.

Pastor C, as he was fondly called, took her aside after the service. She told him exactly what had happened. He noticed that she frequently mentioned Simon and asked if she could bring him to fellowship and she promised to. He asked her to be glad, that God was in control; but she told him of her fears. How difficult it had become to walk alone at night. He encouraged her to let the word of God heal her heart as she had just gone through a traumatic experience.

Though he did not tell her about it, he remembered the day he ran into a 200 level student at about 1:00 am near the science faculty. The path was lonely and she had just been raped by two boys she could not identify and was trying to get herself together in the dead of the night when he got there. He remembered her screams and questions to God, her regret and wishes to die on that day. He had taken her up as a mentee. It had been hard to preach salvation to her at first, but with much prayers and many visits, she had accepted Jesus and was growing every day. He knew Chito's pain was temporary and needed her to know that. She thanked him and went back with Lara to the hostel, praying that people would forget about her episode so they would stop asking about it.

Though she wanted to, she could not tell Pastor C what was really going on with Simon, her emotions were growing and her fears were still alive. Lara went alone to read at night because Chito could not imagine herself going out at night anymore with anyone else but Simon. Any chirp from a cricket or buzz from a mosquito made her cringe in fear, she even cried like a baby when she watched a movie in Simon's room about a girl who had been raped by her uncle and could not tell anyone. For weeks she cried for no reason with reassurances from Simon and Lara.

When she was with Simon, he would take her for walks, telling her she had to deal with the fear. In the room, Lara would play music to soothe her. Gradually, the fear began to fade away and she resumed some regular activities but they agreed to remain in the students' halls of residence and forget about getting accommodation elsewhere.

She could not understand though, why she felt safe with Simon. She would think back and imagine the worst, what would have happened if Simon had not shown up. Every guy was a suspect, every dark place was unsafe, and walking alone was unhealthy. Remembering the past was troubling, the future seemed bleak. She hoped for a miracle. One that would help her put everything that happened behind her.

$\sim\sim\sim\sim\sim$

About three weeks after the school episode, her mother called to say she wanted to see her.

"Will daddy be there too?" she asked in fear.

"No dear! It's just me."

"Okay. When, what time?" she asked, eager for the meet.

"Wednesday, about ten in the morning."

Chito guessed that the timing was to enable her dad go off to work so she would be alone with her mother. It was two days away and she began looking forward to it, excited to have a special time with a parent, even if her dad would not give her audience.

She planned to copy the note for the 10:00 am class from Lara. She packed up a few things and a pair of earrings she had kept for her mother from the gifts she had received from Lara's fiancé.

She left the school compound at 9:00 am so she would be on time. As she got on and off the buses, she thought about her life and the issues she wished she could correct.

As she walked down the street to her house, she couldn't help but think of what her dad would have done if he were there. She expected the worst; she remembered what he had told her at the hospital. It hurt her that she did not have a dad whose shoulder she could cry on. One she could run to and tell her deepest fears. A father she could trust to tell her the difference between a good guy and a bad guy. One she was sure would protect her any day. She wished she had a mother who was not too afraid of her dad to be there for her. She felt trapped, found it difficult to pray, but knew that someday it would be okay.

Stepping out of her own world, she looked up to see the gate to her house. She knocked and Adamu quickly opened the gate, excited to see her.

"*Welicome*," greeted Adamu in his northern accent.

"Thank you," replied Chito as she smiled and asked about his family.

Her mother heard them speak and opened the front

door. Chito walked away from Adamu and towards the woman who was wiping tears from her eyes.

"Mummy, don't cry, I 'm fine," offered an equally teary Chito.

Her mother shut the door and ushered her to a chair. Wiping her face and hugging her as if that would take all the pain away.

"How are you?" she asked.

"I'm scared."

"Scared of what my daughter?"

"I don't know, mummy. I'm scared of guys, of the dark, of everything. People keep looking at me, they think I was really raped."

"Chito, look at me."

She looked at her mother and wiped her face. Ready to listen to some soothing advice.

"Sometimes life deals you an unexpected blow. But when it comes, you have to find a way to deal with it. Chito they did not succeed, did they?"

"No mummy."

"Thank God for that. How did you stop them?"

"My friend came and they ran away."

"Praise God you had a friend there, my daughter. Do you know how many girls are raped daily? How many lives have been affected by rape? Even though I know that God can heal those who are raped, I'm glad you didn't have to go through the trauma. Thank God for your life every day, knowing that the God who kept you that day will keep you always. You cannot stop people from spreading rumours, but you can determine how you will respond to the rumours."

Chito was glad she came home. She wished she could sleep over and listen to more words of encouragement, but she didn't want to see her dad for any reason because she knew he would be upset with her. Her mother knew that as well, although they did not speak of it, so she did not try to make her stay.

As she ate the delicious meal of pounded yam and white soup, she missed home the more. She wondered if her parents would have treated her differently if she had not been their only child.

"Mummy, is there still soup?"

"I knew you would ask, I have already packed a bowl for you."

Chito hugged her. "Hope the meat is plenty like this one?"

Her mother simply laughed and admonished her for her excessive love of meat.

Chito pushed the comment aside and continued licking her soup and eating the numerous pieces of meat her mother had plated for her.

After eating, she took her plate away and started ransacking the kitchen for anything she could pick. She took garri, yams, tinned tomatoes, rice and bowls of soup and stew.

"When will you start eating beans?"

"Mummy, bean porridge is not nice."

"Then why don't you make moin-moin and akara that you love so much?"

"Mummy, those are difficult to make in school. I buy them when I feel like having them."

"How sure are you that they are made hygienically? Please don't eat everything that is sold. Try to cook as much as you can."

"Mummy, I have never seen anyone soak and wash beans in school."

"Why not? Anyway, be careful. Watch where you eat."

"Okay, mummy."

Her mother was happy to have had some alone time with her daughter, she gave her all the encouragement she could and told her she was not to blame for what had happened to her. She advised her to be careful when she walked alone and told her to always go out at night in tight Denim trousers. This made Chito laugh, she didn't know her mother could say such. It was really funny coming from her but she was glad they'd had the talk.

She went to her room before she left, picked up a few accessories and a novel she had left on her reading desk.

"When next will you come home?" queried her mother, longing for a place in the heart of her daughter who she had abandoned emotionally because of her husband's numerous complaints. "Don't spoil her! Let her cook herself! Must you visit her every day? Is she a baby?" These were all questions she'd had to succumb to, and her only child had become really distant from the mother who bore her. She longed to teach her daughter what she knew. She longed to let her know it was okay. To hold her hand and lead her through life's path, but her husband would not let her. She had consented to believe that a husband was the highest authority and must be obeyed; it was what her mother had taught her and what she believed was right. Until she realised her only child was not receiving the love she deserved and began asking God why her fate was sealed thus.

Chito gave her mum the gift she brought and promised to visit home when she could. As Mrs Chiazor watched her daughter walk out the gate, she knew she had received a new mandate. She would pray for her daughter every day so God could correct every wrong foundation in her life, and pray for herself that God would help her live a fulfilled life, despite the odds.

Chito enjoyed every second she spent at home that day. She was glad to talk with her mother and wondered if she could pour her heart out in full. She didn't want to rush the new love but thought of letting it grow before pouring stuff out to her mother. She had to keep the Simon tale between herself and Lara.

CHAPTER FOUR

Their fellowship had a weekend camp meeting at another higher institution in the same state. Plans had been made, fees had been paid, and they gathered at the school's main gate on a Friday to board a bus to their destination. Chito had invited Simon but he could not make it. Lara was there with her, both girls were eager to get out of the stress-filled semester for a little bit of fun. Chito took cornflakes and sugar while Lara took garri, Milo and milk. They knew they would share everything they took.

Lara was in the catering unit while Chito joined the cleaning unit. They had to work in their different units so most of the time they were apart during the day. They went fishing, had Bible study and prayer sessions as well as sporting competitions. It was a fun-filled trip.

On Sunday evening, the day before departure; after sports and before they went to bed, Chito overhead Lara arguing with someone near the bathroom and rushed over to see what it was about. Sandra had just walked out of the bathroom while a resolute Lara remained there, not saying a word. Chito knew her friend was angry and did not want to talk about it, so she waited until Lara had calmed down enough to narrate her story.

Lara had gone to the bathroom first but Stella had insisted on allowing Sandra, a first-year student, to take a bath first. When she tried to explain that she had been there first, Stella had told her not to let her '*Oyinbo bobo*' get to her head. That had made Lara really upset.

"What is the relationship between coming to the bathroom first and having a boyfriend abroad?" she asked. Chito knew the situation did not demand that response, but also knew it was an age-old issue which she had not told her friend about the first time she'd heard it.

The ears on the walls had heard about the fight and people tried to ask both parties what the issue was, but Lara was in no mood for a fight, she was willing to let it go. When she was done with her bath, she dressed up and walked, along with Chito to sit under the moonlight.

"What is wrong with this Stella? she cried. "Is having a fiancé abroad a medal?"

Chito kept quiet, she knew her friend needed to vent. After she had poured out all her thoughts, Chito told her it would be okay. She reminded her to forgive and let God fight for her. From there the conversation moved to other things until they went to bed.

The next day, before they left, the pastor called all the parties involved and helped them work on their differences. Lara was surprised when Stella came to apologise to her for bringing up an unnecessary issue and seemed to mean it. Chito was also surprised and smiled at Stella when they filed into the bus. She was happy when the driver announced that he needed to change a tyre because when they had wanted to go and see the water spring their pastor had called them to try and resolve their differences.

So this was like a final opportunity for them.

They called Charles, who had gone earlier, to accompany them; and he pulled Toye along, an Engineering student who seemed to always be reading while he walked. They hurried down the walkway until they reached the grassy path that led to the spring. Chito pleaded with them to take quick photos of her and Lara whenever they got to a statue or a place she liked. The guys opted to join in the pictures. It was the first time the girls were seeing a spring, they screamed and laughed like babies who had just been given new toys. They had to pull up their trousers to wade in the water until they got to the spring which was crystal clear.

Lara thought the earth around it was as shallow as it looked, she took a step but was saved by Charles' pull. She was surprised that he had known she was falling in and he confessed to having had the same experience when he got there the first time. They had a great time but soon headed back to the bus so they wouldn't miss it. As they walked, they paired up – Chito and Charles, Lara and Toye.

"Sorry to ask you this, but is it true that you are engaged?" asked Toye.

"My story has gone far and wide," replied Lara.

"Is that a 'yes'?"

"Is it a bad thing?"

"I'm just asking to know, Lara. Nothing more."

"Yes," answered Lara.

"How did you guys meet?" probed Toye.

Lara was stunned, she could not tell how they'd met. All she could remember was that her pastor had asked her to store the number and Dapo had started calling her, then spoke with her parents and his family came to see her family. She suddenly felt that something was wrong with her story. No drama, nothing to hold on to. She felt like a commodity being sold to the highest bidder.

"Lord, please don't let me make a mistake," she whispered.

Toye figured she felt embarrassed by his question and quickly changed the topic so she could relax. They laughed until they got to the bus and met the driver just tightening the knots of the new tyre, they were almost good to go.

Lara and Chito were glad they had taken the trip. In spite of all the drama, it had been a restful weekend.

~~~~~

Simon sat by Chito in class. He had teleported from the back seat to the front. His friends jeered at him but he always had a way of laughing it off.

"*You don turn scholar?*" shouted David from the back, mocking his new position at the front of the class.

"*Na im make me come school na,*" was his response.

"*You sure say no be babe make you remember wetin you come do for school so?*" added Chike, a short and fat Ibo boy who was obviously older than all of them. The whole class burst into laughter, except Chito. She was embarrassed but Simon was so casual about it, he wasn't moved.

"*Many babes dey front now, make you come join,*" continued Simon and the guys laughed again. Lara was uncomfortable sitting beside Chito who knew but could do nothing to make her friend feel better. Lara just looked at her and looked away.

That day, the second lecturer for the day announced a surprise test the moment he walked into class. He gave ten minutes of grace and the class was in disarray as students hurriedly scanned through their notebooks, discussing difficult areas of the coursework. The facilities
~~~~~

did not help the situation, as not all the chairs had desks, so students had to sit close together like stuffed tins of sardines. Simon looked ready as did Chito, Lara and a couple of other students.

Lara could not understand how a guy as playful as Simon could be as intelligent as he was. He did not look serious but was one of the best, like herself and Chito. Before they had got all chummy, he had been a backbencher, but that had not stopped him from coming out tops.

$\sim\sim\sim\sim\sim$

The holidays were fast approaching, Chito was going to spend it with her Uncle's family in Warri. She knew it was going to be a long time before she would see Simon again, but she really longed to be in Warri for her Uncle's sixtieth birthday.

"Where will you spend your holidays?" asked Simon on their way to a fellowship meeting. She had invited him and he had honoured her invitation. She told him it was Warri and noticed he raised an eyebrow but said nothing. Just as she was about to question his response, someone tapped her right shoulder from behind, simultaneously saying, "Hi Chito," as she hurried past. She looked and saw that it was Precious, a fellowship member.

"Hi Precious, where are you rushing to?"

"I'm leading worship tonight, have to make rehearsals, and it's almost time!"

"Okay, I'll see you there, won't you meet Simon, a first-time guest?" she called out to Precious' receding form.

Precious turned and hurried back. "Hello," she said to Simon, reaching out for a handshake.

"Hi," said Simon, taking her hand.

"It will be nice having you in fellowship."

"My pleasure" replied Simon, smiling mischievously.

"Chito, can I go now?" She asked rhetorically as she continued her race for time.

"See ya," Chito called out, giggling.

Chito noticed a change in Simon's mood and asked: "Why are you suddenly quiet?"

He paused and then asked, "Are you ashamed of me?"

"No" she blurted out quickly, though she did not

believe her own answer which she had previously not given much thought.

"You introduced me as a first time guest," he accused as his piercing eyes pinned her with the knowing look a mother gives a child who just faltered.

"That is because you are a first time guest," she said, wondering why he was taking it personally.

"I thought I was your friend," he countered.

"Simon, the opportunity for that will arise some other time. Didn't you see she was in a hurry?" She hoped her closing argument succeeded in shaking off the issue at hand.

Simon gave her another knowing look and they walked quietly the rest of the way.

At that point, Chito accepted that she had gone beyond mere friendship with Simon, but she couldn't confront herself with the truth. Her mind told her a lie and she accepted it. "How can I think of him as a boyfriend?" she thought. She could not explain why she felt the way she did whenever he held her close or planted a kiss on her forehead; those butterflies seemed to be around constantly.

Despite the fact that the thoughts plagued her, she

was very happy that Simon had agreed not to go against her wishes; he remained a sweetheart but respected her Christian values. The only challenge she had was that she could not talk to anyone about it, not even Lara. Chito could not imagine speaking to any backbiting sister in fellowship or the sisters' leader because she knew they would smile at her but in her absence, wash her with their mouths and hang her out to dry.

She attended fellowship meetings for the rest of the semester like she was not there. She loved God but didn't understand how she could serve him as she should with all the people that seemed to be the standard around her. She loved Simon's way and prayed earnestly for God to minister to him so he would accept Christ in addition to his niceness. He didn't force her to do what she wouldn't; like attend parties, but still, he doted on her like a butterfly would a flower.

~~~~~

"Chito, are you still going to Warri?" asked Simon as they walked back from class after their final paper for the
~~~~~

semester. She answered in the affirmative, wondering why he raised a question he knew the answer to. He looked at her again, unable to hide his enthusiasm as his smile almost reached from ear to ear.

"What now!" Chito pressured until he eventually told her he lived in Warri. She felt like jumping as he was still smiling, he just walked close and hugged her, kissing her forehead again, as had become the custom since she told him she couldn't go beyond that point. He knew Benin City so well that she had not known he lived out of town.

Chito wanted to tell Lara about her 'Simon discovery' as they packed for the break, but pushed the idea aside, wondering what the consequences would be. She'd had a heart to heart with Lara the day before about Lara's troubles and didn't want to confuse the situation.

"Chito, he says he is not sure he can come to Nigeria until after about seven years," a frantic Lara had said, looking downcast as she folded clothes into her bag.

"Seven years?" exclaimed Chito, wondering how that would work out. "You are now in year three. There's just one session left to be through with school then go for NYSC. After that will you sit down for another five years, not knowing if this man will return?" At this point, Lara started crying. Chito couldn't believe it. "Lara, will you really wait?" Chito asked, amazed but sorry for her friend.

"I don't want to miss God's will for my life," cried Lara.

Chito simply put her arm around Lara's shoulder as her friend wept. She didn't know what to say to her. She couldn't tell if it was Lara's tale that got her dumbfounded or her own secret that she couldn't share. But she felt Lara had had her fair share of pain and didn't want to add to it.

CHAPTER FIVE

Chito's parents were surprised at her short stay at home, she was in a hurry to get to her uncle's house. They wondered at first but later gave in, believing she wanted to make the most of her holiday.

She got to Warri at about 2.30 pm the next Saturday. Her cousin, Kome, came to pick her up from the park. He was a six-footer and beside him, she always felt like a dwarf at five feet four inches. It made her dread his hugs. He was the first son born to her mother's brother after 12 years of marriage. He had a younger brother, Tega, who was fifteen years old. Kome was twenty. They were also believers and Chito was very close to Kome because they were in the same age group.

As they drove home, her phone rang, it was Simon. "Yeah, I'll ask for the address and send to you. Bye!" she said to him.

"Hmmm?" Kome murmured.

She eyed him, asking why he had said that. He just laughed and reminded her that her phone's speaker had been on. She bit her lip in regret because it meant he heard the 'I love you' and 'I miss you' Simon had said.

"What are you not telling me?" he asked.

"Don't worry, he's just a friend," Chito defended and he just smiled. She remembered their first bonding experience, the day they got baptised in the Holy Ghost. They had been at Kome's family church in Warri, and their bond was beyond that of mere cousins, he was like her blood brother.

Things went on as usual; Chito sent her new address to Simon who promised to visit soon. Uncle Dafe and Aunty Rose, Kome's parents, were out of the country and would be back in a few days so Kome went shopping with Chito so they could cook and stock up the house before his parents arrived. They cooked ohwo, pepper soup and Edikang-Ikong soup as well as some stew to store in the freezer for their return. Kome was an exceptional cook, his mother had taught him well.

The next day, Simon visited and Chito introduced him to Kome who was the only one at home, and Simon offered to take her to know his place. When she told Kome, he refused, saying he would take her there himself some other time. She pleaded and he eventually let her go, but she knew he was not happy about it.

Simon drove her through his estate gate. She couldn't believe he was from a wealthy family because he never really acted as rich as he truly was. Her surprise grew to awe when they got to the front of his house. His home was lovely. They went in and he introduced her to his older brother who welcomed her enthusiastically, calling her the babe who made his brother sane. She felt proud and surprised at the same time because she hadn't realised she was adding value to Simon in any way.

His brother confirmed that he didn't attend late-night parties anymore because his girlfriend didn't like them. She felt proud, and as his brother left them home alone, she got really uncomfortable with her feelings towards him. He microwaved some stew and chicken which they ate with the rice in the cooker. He served some juice and they watched a movie.

After eating, Simon moved really close to Chito as they sat on the sofa, chatting her up and asking where she would love him to take her. She asked God under her breath to help her stay strong, then she told Simon that she didn't know too many places in Warri except places she had visited when she was much younger and he promised her the vacation of a lifetime. He was touching her hair and she didn't know what to do but stare at him as those butterflies came back alive in her stomach. Just then, Kome called. "Hello!" Chito said with a knowing look as if he could see her. "Chito, are you done?"

She told him she was still at Simon's place, but he said he was in the area and thought he could take her home.

Simon told Chito her cousin was being really protective but it was okay. As she put her shoes back on, he rushed to the room and brought a wrapped gift that he wanted her to open when she got home.

Chito said a quick thank you, feeling bad for always

being on the receiving end. That got her thinking of what to get for Simon as they walked out of his door.

Kome had gotten the address before she left the house so he came to the right place without much ado. They said their goodbyes and Simon gave Chito a side hug without the forehead kiss. She sat uncomfortably in the front with Kome and he said a smiling goodbye to Simon but froze immediately they drove off. Tears gathered in his eyes and Chito couldn't help but wonder what the problem was.

"Why are you crying?" she asked, getting emotional herself. He swiped an arm across his eyes and parked the car. Chito smelt trouble and didn't know how to escape.

"What has gotten into your head?" he asked, as tears still struggled to make their way out of his ducts. She knew exactly what he meant, she felt the pangs herself but they had woven around her a basket she could not get out of. She was quiet as a dove and he turned to and away from her intermittently.

At this point, all she could do was pour out her soul in honesty. "Kome, please pray for me because I don't know what I am doing." She told him about the near-rape case and how Simon had been there for her. How she fought thoughts of becoming like her mother and like Lara who was in a fix and all the confusion with gossip in the church. At this point, she was in tears.

He looked at her calmly. "It's the end times, sis. These things are bound to happen. But the solution is not running from God, it is in running *to* him." As he said this, fresh tears ran down her cheeks but he continued as if he didn't see them. "When last did you take a day out to fast and pray to God concerning these challenges? You are picking out your own solution, and what does the Bible say? Except the Lord builds a house, you build in vain."

The words pierced through her heart like a sword. "So what do I do now?" she asked in desperation. "I love Simon very much and he loves me too. I need him to get born again so we can truly be together."

He grinned at that. "You want to tell God what is right? Remember he doesn't share his glory." At that, he took her hands in his and began to pray in the spirit. The presence of God was so strong that she felt it. She remembered Kome's Sunday school teacher telling them not to be unequally yoked, but somehow she was dancing in that direction.

They drove home afterwards and got home towards evening. It was a prayer meeting day at Kome's church so they went together and it was truly refreshing. Immediately after, Chito felt like she should let go of Simon altogether, it was so strong that she didn't remind him of her uncle's party that Saturday, but because she had mentioned it earlier, he showed up.

~~~~~

Uncle Dafe and his wife arrived two days before his big day. They had already made preparatory arrangements before they left, so they didn't have much to do except follow up on existing preparations and make the kids fill the gift bags with souvenirs they had brought from the US.

"Chito don tall like Iroko tree," commented her uncle regarding her stature. Not that she was extremely tall, but she had been very short as a little girl, so no one expected her to turn out five feet four. For her, it was a great achievement. Everyone laughed at her and reminded her of her childhood.

"Dad, do you remember how she couldn't reach for
~~~~~

cereal in the kitchen cabinet?" Kome asked his dad who burst out in a fresh bout of laughter.

Chito remembered and laughed too. "Kome, I was just being civil."

"Civil?" Kome asked rhetorically amidst good-natured chuckles.

"Okay now, everybody please leave my Chito baby for me. Soon now one bobo will show up for marriage."

"God forbid," exclaimed Chito.

"Which God?" asked her uncle. "You are a girl, you better start thinking of marriage."

"Uncle it's not yet time." Chito giggled as she spoke.

"Please let this girl grow up and live first. Chito please I'm not saying wait forever, but there's no hurry." Her aunt patted her back affectionately.

"Thanks, aunty."

Her uncle just made a funny face and left them in the sitting room.

~~~~~

The party was awesome; in attendance were two of
~~~~~

Uncle Dafe's primary school mates and lots of acquaintances from here and there. Everything was lovely, the MC, music, food and all. It was obvious that a lot of time and money had been spent on the spectacular event. As usual, Simon's presence was noticed even by Uncle Dafe. "Who is that *mucheche*?" he whispered into Chito's ear as she served him a salad at the end of the event. She simply blushed and ran away while he said a few words to his wife. She turned around to see them watching her with big smiles.

As she walked Simon back to his car, Uncle Dafe intercepted them and introduced himself. Chito braced herself for the confrontation she had been trying to avoid. Surprisingly, he sounded pleased and asked to see Simon again the next week. Chito was glad for one ally.

Every time Kome tried to talk to Simon whenever he came over to see her, Chito brought up something else or hurried Simon out of the house.

"Chito, this guy is picking you up a lot," observed Kome.

"He is teaching me to swim," she responded. "It's mainly Shell Club we go to, we only go to other places once in a while. You can come and watch me, I'll soon swim like a fish," she sounded excited about her new pastime.

"Can you float yet?" he asked, remembering how hydrophobic she had been when they were younger.

"Float?" she huffed. "I can swim now."

He was surprised at her speed, happy that she could finally swim but not pleased that it was Simon who had taught her.

~~~~~

"Chito, relax," was Simon's soothing phrase because she had been shaking like a leaf, apprehensive of swimming without her life jacket for the first time. Then he just smiled. That smile always won her heart and got right to the core of her being. It disarmed her enough to temporarily forget the fear.

"Will you swim with me?" she asked the still smiling Simon, fighting the fear that shook her visibly.

"Baby, you don't need me," was his confident response, and she looked from him to the water before deciding to try. She swam gently, as slow as she could but when she got close to the deep part, she quickly made a U-turn, only to face Simon who had been moving quietly
~~~~~

behind her. He swam back with her to the start point and she rushed out as fast as she could; glad about the swim, but eager to be out.

"That was great," uttered a proud Simon, as he rushed out of the water as well. He wrapped her in a hug to celebrate the victory. It was awkward to feel his wet skin against her body. She froze because she felt vulnerable, enjoying the warmth as the butterflies returned. And then he kissed her right there, on the lips.

Like a flash of lightning, she broke free and ran, not responding to the shouts of "Chito!" behind her. She remembered his promise to never push her beyond what she was comfortable with and was concerned that if he broke his promise with this, she couldn't trust him to not go further. But beyond his actions, she didn't trust herself either. She was upset that he had broken their promise but was scared that she would soon defect to his way of thinking.

Simon was a faster runner and caught up with her quickly. She flung a hand out at him when he tugged at her to halt her flight.

"Don't come close to me," she threatened.

"Why are you being timid, Chito? It was a mistake," replied Simon. "I'm really sorry, I promise it won't happen again."

She packed her things up and got outside before she remembered she had left her purse at home. Embarrassed, she walked to the car and stood at the passenger's side while Simon hurriedly dressed up and joined her.

"I'm sorry," he repeated over and over as they drove, but she didn't trust him anymore.

"Chito, it was just a kiss," he said again as he dropped her off. "I love you and I really don't see anything wrong with an accidental kiss. I agreed to the sex no-no, not kissing."

Chito was conflicted. She grouped it all together, so that may have confused Simon, but she didn't feel ready to deal with the issue so she just told him she wanted a break.

"It's not fair!" he reacted. "Chito, we can walk through this. You know how much you mean to me."

She stepped out of his car when he dropped her off, ignoring his plea, listening to her own heart this time.

~~~~~
~~~~~

"Simon has not been around in a while," observed Kome rhetorically.

"Yes," was Chito's flat response, as if she didn't care. She continued sweeping the floor to the guest room where she slept as if his statement meant nothing. He raised his brows, looking at her with concern and love. She knew he loved her like she was his baby sister. It was so funny because they were the same age, yet he cared for and protected her as though she was younger. Chito dropped the broom, feeling destabilised. She sat on the floor and started to cry. Kome went to sit by her. He put his hand on her shoulder and she cried even harder, leaning into him as he wound his arms around her.

"Chito, talk to me," he pressed, eager to understand her pain. She felt so choked up that she could only cry until she felt relieved. She raised her head and leaned back against the wall while Kome took his hands away, sitting close but leaning on the bed.

"Why were you crying?" he asked again, and this time she knew she had to tell the truth, she was tired of the deception.

"Simon kissed me by the pool," she said amidst

tears. "Can you imagine, he kissed me openly in front of people?" she fumed. Tears dropped again, but Kome just stared at her.

"Won't you say something?" she blurted out, transferring her aggression to the innocent Kome, but he was silent. She waited a while, he still said nothing so she picked up the broom and continued sweeping.

Kome did not revisit the issue for a while that day, he went out to see some friends and came back later in the afternoon. He cooked, kept some food for his parents in the food flask and served up food to everyone at home.

"Kome I'm not taking food from you until we talk about this morning. There's a gulf between us and we need to bridge it. Please say something."

"I will, but can we do that later?"

"Okay," she said, collecting the food he had dished out for her and going over to the table to have her meal, but he did not join them at the table.

"Why is Kome not having lunch?" Tega asked, surprised that his brother was skipping lunch.

"I'm not sure," was her response, but she couldn't get the thought out of her mind. The possibility that she was responsible for his pain burnt her with guilt. She lost her appetite. "Tega, do you want more rice?"

"With the meat, yes."

"Who will give you meat?" She responded, shoving the protein into her mouth and taking her food to the kitchen. She covered the food in the plate with a plastic bowl and leaving it in the kitchen, went to Kome's room to knock. Kome did not answer so she opened the door and saw him on his knees leaning over with his face pressed to the bed and she knew he was praying for her.

She felt a pang of guilt. "God, I've not prayed for myself or anyone else in a while," she whispered, realising how she had become possessed by Simon. Wondering when last she had taken out her Bible to study, she broke down in tears and ran into her room.

"Please help me!" she cried to God, "Even if it means hurting me. Why do I feel tied to him?" She cried and prayed for a while, then thanked God for his mercy and grace to deliver her.

As she folded the washed clothes that were on the bed, Kome walked in and sat on the bed to help her. When they were done, she put the clothes away.

"Chito, please sit down," he asked gently and her mind went wild, wondering what he would say.

"I hope he won't be too angry with Simon," she thought.

Calmly, he said, "Chito, I wasn't surprised that Simon kissed you, but what hurt me was the fact that your concern was not that you were even dating an unbeliever or kissing an unbeliever, but that he kissed you in public. Would it have been okay in his house?" This time his voice was raised, "Chito I know you do not intend to have sex before you are married, but if you continue like this, I think you will."

"I won't," she blurted out, "God forbid."

"You are already unequally yoked, Chito. It's a gradual process." He paused and then added, "and subtle too."

They were both quiet, only the squeaky sound of the ceiling fan filled the room. She thought of a way out but found none she liked. She knew speaking with anyone from her dad's church was not safe, as the information could get back to her dad and he would kill her. Lara had her own issues which she didn't want to add to, so Kome was her best option.

"I know I should not date an unbeliever but everything happened so fast I couldn't even think. I just don't want to fall for a guy like my father or Lara's Dapo who I don't think loves his fiancée and is a crook. Do you know she doesn't even know what being in love is? But her pastor thinks he is God's choice for her and she has accepted it. I need someone who can love me and make me laugh while I serve God."

"I understand that perfectly, and I believe that is God's will for us all, but do you really think Simon is that guy?" He paused as if to let it sink in properly, then continued. "He kissed you, Chito. In public. Do you think he won't break his promise again?"

"I don't know if I can break up with him, Kome."

"Even after this?" He wondered what was wrong with her. "Have you ever preached Christ to him?"

"He knows my Do's and Don'ts," she hedged, but he just shook his head.

"Your Dos and Don'ts? Are you Christ?"

"I know I'm not," she retorted, "but I let him know I'm a Christian and that keeps him in check."

"I can see how much 'in check' he is," was Kome's response and it stung her hard.

"Chito, you are walking away from God and you need to retrace your steps. Let God in and then you can have the grace to say no to sin."

She knew he was right, but still tried to defend herself anyway. "I pray for him to get born again."

Kome picked up the bottle of groundnut on her table and reminded her that she was supposed to be an epistle. "Simon is supposed to become a Christian when he sees you, but it is now the other way around. You are being enticed to sin."

"I believe God will change him so I would not have to break up with him," she said dreamily. Kome laughed heartily and looked at her pitifully.

"I thought I told you that God does not play by our rules?"

She was silent again, impregnated by guilt, heavy with fear. Fear of the unknown. Fear of what would become of her if Simon chose to leave her. Fear of what she would do if he kissed her again. Fear of what she would do if her father found out. Tangible fear struck her and she knew she needed a way out.

"I will leave on Saturday," she said to Kome.

"That is just two days away," he pointed out. "Why the sudden change? You said you were leaving next week."

"I need to clear my head."

"I understand," said Kome, taking some more groundnuts from the bottle.

Chito looked at the bottle in his hand and realised that it was almost empty.

"Do you want to finish my groundnuts?" she accused him and he held it away so she couldn't reach it. She got up to fight for what was hers and he stood up, holding it above his head. She climbed the bed, and he walked towards the wardrobe.

"Give it to me!" she screamed at him, but he was having a good laugh, pouring groundnuts into his hands and stuffing them quickly into his mouth.

Tega who was passing by saw the little drama and joined in. "Bros, give me small," he called to his brother who poured some into his hands. They kept moving the bottle above Chito's head, pouring into their palms and stuffing their mouths like little babies until there were about five seeds left.

"Oya take now! I left some for you," Kome said, handing the bottle over to her, with satisfaction and mischief written all over his face.

"What did you leave?" Chito yelled, refusing to collect the bottle. The boys laughed, but she knew she couldn't face Kome so she ran after Tega who quickly locked himself in his room. Then she walked back to her room where Kome was waiting for her. She gave him a knock on his head and he playfully tried to retaliate until they fell to the floor laughing.

The day's prank reminded her of their days as kids when they would play all day and pray together before bedtime, praying in the spirit like they had been taught to in church. As if he read her thoughts, Kome placed his hands on her shoulders and began to pray in tongues. She joined him, praying in the heavenly language because she knew human wisdom could not help her out of her predicament.

"Kome, please don't stop praying for me," she said when they were done praying.

"I won't," he said, knowing he had a new prayer point. He left a while later to watch a match with Tega in their room. As he walked out, Chito heard a still small voice in her heart say, 'Fight for your faith the way you fought for your groundnuts.'

She recognised that voice, the voice of the comforter, the teacher. "I have to break up with Simon," she whispered. "God help me."

~~~~~

"I am missing your trouble already," Chito said to Kome as he drove her to the park.

"My trouble or yours?" He grinned. "Hmm," he sighed. "No more market partner for me." They laughed because stocking up the house was his responsibility and Chito always helped him.

"Thanks for leading me back on track."

"Thank God for his grace, I was scared you were gone from grace."

"Naaaaaa. I'm back, bro."

"Welcome back, sis," he said as he drove into the park.

They got her ticket and she had to wait for only four more passengers before her bus departed.
~~~~~

~~~~~

Being home was depressing. Chito's dad made them read the Bible and listen to him from 5:00 to 7:00 am every day. He always preached and never let her mother or anyone else contribute. Chito couldn't understand why.

"Does God speak to men only?" she thought. "Who spoke to me then?" Chito knew what she had heard, that it was real.

Her dad would go on and on about how people adored him in church but his family didn't. He asked Chito why she was not in the choir or among those cleaning the church. He told her she didn't act like a pastor's kid. He always blamed her for one thing or the other, a single conversation could not be held without him comparing her to another pastor's daughter or deacon's son.

Chito just wanted to be herself. Oddly enough, she did not get born again in her dad's church but in Kome's. Secretly, she believed that if her dad's church had been the only church in existence, she might never have given her heart to Jesus.
~~~~~

That day, Lara came to see her at home, a big relief from the humdrum daily routine. Chito was in the kitchen, serving up some of the food she had cooked when Simon called. Lara saw the incoming call and brought the phone to her in the kitchen. Chito smiled as she took the phone and turned away, effectively dismissing Lara who went back to the sitting room. She didn't want Lara to know the current situation.

"I've missed you," Simon declared barely five seconds into the call.

A chill travelled down her spine, she missed him too. She was not happy about the kiss but she wanted to see him although she had vowed to end the relationship earlier.

When she went back into the sitting room Lara asked how he was. Chito replied that he was fine and asked how Dapo was.

Lara revealed that she was considering breaking her engagement but didn't know what her parents and church would think of her. "Do you miss him?" Chito asked.

"Well, I can't say that I miss him, but whenever I see couples together, I wish he lived closer. Someone told me recently about an aunt who had been married to a man who was based abroad, and for ten years she was unable to get a visa to join him. She ended up getting a divorce and moving on with her life."

"What? That's terrible!"

"Right? I'm sort of worried that could be my fate," Lara confided, moving her fork in her barely touched meal.

"Lara, I feel you, but I must be honest with you. I don't think this is the best relationship for you. It just feels like you're a chicken tied up in the backyard, waiting to be slaughtered. You should feel like a bird, you need to fly."

She laughed at the imagery. "Yes, but I don't want to fly like you to a guy like Simon. Seriously, Chito, I'm not comfortable with you and Simon, I know he likes you and you like him, but I'm scared for you."

"Simon kissed me," she blurted out, looking at her friend with stony eyes, waiting for a jab or a spank.

"When?" she asked in shock.

Chito told her about the Warri charade, ensuring that she left no detail out because she was done with the lies. She just wanted the truth to set her free.

"What will you do now?" Lara asked when the tale was done.

"I'll break up with him," Chito said with painful resolve.

"Let's both break up," she suggested. "I don't think we are in the right if we feel so wrong."

Chito confessed that she knew she had to break up with Simon, but after hearing his voice on the phone, she wasn't sure she could bring herself to do it.

"I've been thinking," murmured Lara, "I think we are concentrating on our ability. I was listening to a preacher on TV last week and he said a lot of Christians fail because they don't pray about their challenges until the mountains move. It made me think of my situation. Everything seems to be against me; my relationship, my church, my family. I don't know how to tell them I want to end my relationship since they believe it is God's will for my life. I don't even pray about it. How can I fight this battle myself except God helps me? Same for you Chito, you want to end things with Simon but you can't bring yourself to do it. Let's pray, joh!"

And that was how they held hands and prayed until they felt the presence of God. It was the best time Chito had ever spent with Lara and she wondered why they had never really prayed together before. They normally spent most of the time sharing their woes; Lara would complain about her relationship and Chito would whine about her parents.

Every day she picked Simon's calls, Chito told herself she was going to break up with him. But she could never do it. She shared the challenge with Kome and Lara over the phone and they advised her to keep on praying.

God came through for Lara, she succeeded in ending her engagement, but Chito was still hoping for her own answer.

CHAPTER SIX

Two weeks before school was to re-open, Chito got an urgent call from Stephen, Simon's brother. He said Simon had been involved in a car accident on his way to school and that he had a laceration on his head. They didn't know if he would survive and he begged her to come over to Warri to try and save Simon emotionally.

Chito was at a crossroad, she didn't know what to do. She called Lara and Kome. Kome went there to see him and told her that Simon was in a critical state and unconscious. She cried for two days, she could not get herself together.

Her mom tried to find out why she was crying.

When Chito insisted that she would be okay, her mother asked if she wanted to go back to Warri before school resumed. It was a miracle, for she had not known how to take permission without lying or implicating herself. She was really glad to leave the house. Her mom knew she had been enduring her dad's dictatorship and helped her leave the next day.

The trip seemed longer than usual. Chito counted trees, traffic lights, bridges, hoping to arrive sooner. She wanted to see Simon, she didn't want him to pass on before she got there and she prayed he wouldn't die. As the bus finally approached Effurun junction, she gathered her stuff quickly, zipping up her bag, anxious to come down as the driver turned into the park.

She sighted Kome walking towards the bus. She had given him the name of the transport company and the bus number so he knew it was her bus. She gave him a hurried hug, asking immediately about Simon, who she had instructed him to visit regularly. He just smiled and walked to the car, ignoring her chatter. They got in and started driving, Chito felt very strange and scared.

"Kome, is he okay?" she asked, starting to cry.

There was so much pressure welled up inside her that she almost could not breathe.

"Simon has regained consciousness but he's still a bit feeble. He has been asking for you."

Chito felt warm inside when she heard that. But she knew she was in a fix because she needed to break up with Simon. She didn't know when she said out loud, "I'll break up when he is better."

Kome's laughter startled her out of her thoughts but she couldn't take her words back. He glanced at her and said, "All I can do now is pray for you, I don't know what else to do."

She caught the flash of pain in his eyes, the only person who really cared about her, the brother she'd never had. She wondered how he put up with her. If her dad knew about Simon, she was sure he'd never talk to her again, like the girl in church who had been caught with a guy she was not married to. She had repented and said she was sorry. She ended the relationship with the guy, but Chito's dad always looked the other way when he saw her. He had treated her like a plague-infected human until she left the church.

They drove straight to the hospital and Chito asked Kome why he checked on Simon when he didn't approve of the relationship.

"I am a child of God. I saw someone who needed help and I helped him. I will preach Christ to him when he is stable," he said calmly. "Why are you smiling at me like that?"

"If you get Simon born again, I can marry him."

"Chito, you're still worshipping yourself." He shook his head but smiled indulgently.

Chito hissed and folded her hands. "You're just jealous."

At the hospital she practically jumped out of the car, walking as fast as she could behind Kome to Simon's room.

She saw Simon and broke down in tears, she couldn't say hello. It was much worse than they had said. She ran to his side and he squeezed her hand. There was a bandage around his head and his left leg was elevated. His brother gave her a chair. She sat and placed her head on the bed with her hand still in his. He was in pain but still his jovial self.

"You dey come greet me with cry?" he asked playfully.

She still couldn't look up, so he placed a hand on her head and said with the weakest tone she had ever heard from him, "Chito please stop crying."

She felt movement in the room and knew it was Kome who had left because Simon had started smoothing back the hair on her head. She knew her cousin could not stand any appearance of sin, even if it concerned her.

She felt terrible for Kome, but she also felt sorry for Simon. His brother had said he needed all the emotional support he could get and she had decided to stay by him until he was okay, before ending things.

Simon's injuries healed quickly, but his leg didn't. The doctor said it hadn't been well taken care of at the first hospital he had been rushed to, so it developed an infection which was proving difficult to treat. He was on antibiotics, but the leg was still not healing. Whenever they dressed the wounds Simon cried like a baby and hit the bed like he wanted to die. Chito felt sorry for him but she prayed earnestly and believed he would be okay.

The school lecturers were on strike to settle some internal issues with the vice-chancellor, giving Simon ample time to recover. After a month, the doctor discharged him, asking him to come for dressing every day. He then told him that if after a while the leg didn't heal, he would advise amputation from the knee so that the other parts of the leg and body would not be affected.

Simon was upset when he heard this. He really couldn't walk so it was more difficult to contain his emotions, he would throw things at the wall and scream, "God, why?"

Chito encouraged him and stood by him just as he had done for her. She kept praying for God to have mercy on him.

Her parents soon came to Warri for a week to witness the commissioning of a branch of their church. Chito stayed away from Simon's place the entire time they were around.

"When are you coming to Benin?" her dad asked the day her parents were ready to depart.

"I'm not sure yet."

He was surprised at her response but he didn't speak further.

That morning, he had shared about youthful

exuberance, stating that girls and boys needed to take their proposed spouses to their parents before asking or responding to a proposal because the parents were still wiser and would make the right choice for the children.

Kome and Chito glanced at each other because the pastor who preached in Kome's church had addressed it the previous day, stating that marriage was between two people and that while one shouldn't dishonour the parents but at the same time people should be sure that whoever they married was a believer they were comfortable with and had rest in their spirit about. He also said they should let their pastor know their choice.

Chito sighed as she thought of the numerous engagements her dad had broken up because the prospective spouses were not members of his church, or those he forced to marry, telling them that he would revoke their positions in the church if they didn't oblige.

The word of God was indeed a powerful tool, some used it to their own glory, but others to the glory of God. When Kome's pastor had asked them to pray, Chito bowed her head and asked God to help her please him in all her ways and not please man. To give her wisdom in her dealings with Simon.

She finally went to see him when her parents left. She was enthusiastic but Kome wasn't. She paid off the bike man at the gate and started her trek into the estate since Kome had refused to take her. Stephen drove past and reversed, she didn't even see him until he was right beside her. He took her to their home, telling her that she had abandoned Simon.

Chito explained that they had been communicating all through and he thanked her for all she had done for his brother, saying he prayed she would be the one Simon married. She felt good, but she had never thought of marriage before then.

Simon was awake and watching a movie. When she entered he held her and kissed her, with his brother still at the door. She was a bit uneasy but she let him. She couldn't imagine fighting him off at a time like that. But before God, she felt like trash. His brother asked if Simon needed him to get anything and Simon asked for a bottle of brandy.

"Brandy! Why?" Chito asked in shock as his brother walked away.

"Don't look so shocked. It's just a way to drown

the pain."

"You don't need it, don't you have drugs for pain?"

"It's not the same, Chito. I just need to be free for some time. I need to forget my problems. I have a doctor's appointment in three days' time to decide if I will need to…if amputation is the next step."

Her heartbeat increased, a million times faster than the clock ticking on Simon's wall.

He begged her to bear with him, that he was confused, he felt bed-ridden because he could not move around freely.

Chito felt sorry for him, she knew he needed Jesus, but who was she to speak about that?

Simon kissed her again, and again then held her close. He broke down and cried like a baby and she hugged him, crying as well. He touched her, slipping his hands into her blouse, and she let him, enjoying the newness of the sensations running through her.

Just then, her phone rang. It was Kome and he said he was on his way to Simon's place. She thanked God for the call because, with the way she had been feeling, she wouldn't have been able to stop Simon. In fact, she wanted more; he sparked up a flame in her and now a slow fire was burning, hot!

It just had to be God who saved her from incineration, she thought, but why had he?

Kome came in about twenty minutes later and met them talking. Stephen came in with the brandy and Kome asked why Simon was drinking. He told Kome about the amputation and Kome told him he did not need brandy but Jesus. Simon laughed and said he didn't think God had him in his good books, but Kome encouraged him saying that if he accepted Christ, he would have the right to God's grace and power.

Before Chito's eyes, Simon accepted Jesus. He said the sinners' prayer and promised Kome that if he could recover from the accident totally without needing an amputation, he would truly follow Jesus all his days. Kome prayed for him, as heartily as he prayed for Chito when he knew she was going astray. He laid his hands on Simon's leg and prayed for the mercy and grace of God. After the prayers, they chatted for a while before Kome insisted that they had to leave.

The drive home was silent. Chito was lost in

thought. She felt bad, but why? Did she feel bad that Simon got born again or did she feel guilty about kissing him and letting him touch her beneath her clothes? It could even have been the pangs of guilt because she had not been the one who got Simon born again. Whatever it was, she couldn't bring herself to say anything to Kome.

She looked up at the birds flying in the sky and wondered when life would be that easy again. She longed to kiss Simon again and didn't know what to do about her break up decision. She felt trapped.

She went on her knees that night and prayed earnestly as she used to when she was twelve years old. She wanted God to help her make a choice but she needed his grace this time.

When she filled Lara in on what was happening Lara asked her to let God have his way.

Have his way with what? She blamed God for letting her path cross Simon's when it did, but was it really God's fault? She had known Simon was an unbeliever, but why could she not have pushed him off when he kissed her the second time, or the third? She was learning his ways, becoming like him, longing for him. At that thought, she remembered the still small voice the day Kome and Tega had eaten her groundnuts, God had instructed her to fight for her faith the way she fought for her groundnuts.

She had never really had to fight for her faith before. She got born again and was always in church with one activity or another. She had been so busy for God that she hadn't known there were foundational truths she needed to get into her spirit and soul. Being in school had exposed her to a lot of people and activities she was not used to, and she had been powerless before them, powerless before Simon. She knew she was on the wrong path but she just couldn't turn away.

"God, what is wrong with me?" she murmured.

She knew God still loved her because the last time she had been with Simon she had been willing to give in but Kome's call had saved the day.

God knew how terrible she would have felt if she let Simon go all the way.

~~~~~

Simon returned from the hospital with good news, he did not need an amputation and he would walk again. He
~~~~~

was exceptionally glad, he even took Kome and Chito out to announce to them that he wanted to keep his vow to God by becoming a real Christian. Kome told him that he was already a real Christian since he had given his life to Christ, but that he needed to read the Bible and pray daily to grow in the spirit and know God more intimately.

Simon took the advice heartily and a part of Chito wished that he was not serious. She could not understand her feelings. She was a believer and was supposed to be happy when someone came into the kingdom, but she wasn't happy that Simon was eager to know God more. She wanted him for herself to fan the flames of lust that had come alive within her. The feeling of being touched, of being held, of being kissed, strange fire.

The week before school finally resumed, Simon came by, more cheerful than ever. He still walked with a stick, but his swag made his limp look cute. Kome, Tega and Chito had been playing a game of Monopoly and did not stop when he came, so he took over recording the scores.

Chito looked at him and was thrilled by his disposition. She couldn't imagine smiling in his predicament but he was still smiling, he was happy. Her heart was shaking, she did not know how to let go of Simon. She had lost her peace concerning him, whenever she was with him, her heart beat faster.

When the game was over, Kome was moving toward the rooms when Simon called him back.

"What does the Bible mean by 'what does it profit a man to gain the whole world and lose his soul'?" He said it innocently, like a child, adding that whenever he saw it his heart beat faster.

Chito laughed, wondering how anyone would not know the meaning of that scripture. But Kome took him aside and explained that he had to let go of earthly pleasures to preserve a pure heart before God, making him fit for heaven.

He thanked Kome and reclined as if in deep thought. Kome asked if something was wrong but he replied in the negative, he just sat, glanced at Chito then continued in thought. The smile on his face was gone, and he opted to leave. It was unusual because he usually stayed longer. Chito wasn't happy but she had to let him go. With the way his mood had changed, she offered to go to his place with him.

In his room, he fell face down on the bed and wept. She was confused. She went close to him and put her hand on his back but he shrugged it off. She felt insulted. She shook him, asking what was wrong and he got up, turning to face her with eyes full of fire. Then he asked the question, the one that made her want to hide her head in shame.

"Chito, have we been on the right track?"

"How?" she asked. Even though she knew exactly what he meant.

"Chito, we've been kissing and I touched you. I fiddled with your body, Chito. Was that right?"

She looked down, unable to give an answer because she knew the truth, the truth that could set her free but she hadn't heeded it. She admired Simon; admired his childlike sincerity. He was sincere with the word; he hadn't seared his heart like she had, explaining sin away just because she did not want to yield to the checks in her heart.

She had known sex was for marriage, but no one had told her about the preliminaries, or that a guy could kiss her to a point where she would be willing to let him do whatever he wanted with her. She hadn't known, and she'd lacked the power to say no because she no longer read her

Bible or prayed daily. She had become cold, ice-cold like that tempting bottle of soda in the arid harmattan season.

"God!" she thought, "what do I do, why do I feel powerless?"

Simon was looking at her like she was a demon, like she was filth.

"Simon, I love you," she cried but he said not a word. He just looked away, deep in thought.

She cried as she moved toward him. He had sat up on the bed, resting his back against the wall. She sat and rested her head on his shoulder. He tried to move but she accused him then.

"You taught me, Simon. I was never so close to a guy before you!" she screamed.

He looked at her intently and said in all sincerity, "I didn't know."

His words felt like a spear driving through her heart with force. She broke down again but this time, he felt guilty, this time he came to her, and held her and kissed her.

"I'm sorry," he said. They hugged.

She cried and he tried to hold her as if it would stop the tears. "I'm sorry," he repeated.

Then she felt guilty, she had made him break his vow. He didn't want her anymore but she had made him, she truly wanted him to know he was to blame. But was he really?

The Holy Ghost had come to teach her the truth but she had not received the lesson, how could she blame him? She packed up her things and was about leaving when he asked, "What do we do?"

She cried in confusion and sat on the floor.

"God saved my leg, I made a vow."

She nodded in response, she knew he wanted to keep to his word but she was his stronghold.

"We can get married now that you are a Christian," she suggested.

He shook his head and said, "I want to stop every wrong thing I'm doing right now to follow God."

She couldn't understand. "You have stopped partying, you don't have sex. What else do you want to stop?"

He held his head in both hands and stretched his other leg to complement the sore one.

"I just wasn't having sex with you, Chito. I was still

having sex with others," he confessed.

A holy fire welled up within her. She lunged at him and tried to fight him, but he shrugged her off and got up, picking up his stick.

She felt dirty, like a muddy lake. She walked out of his room. He tried to call her back, but she didn't respond. She had had enough.

Simon came by the house the next day but Chito didn't come out to see him. Kome tried to call her but she didn't respond. He had a one-on-one with Kome and she could only imagine Kome encouraging him to stay focused on God. She knew he would not water down the truth for anyone, not even her. She knew he would tell Simon it was a trial of his faith. That he would have to take his eyes off Chito and place them on God as his source and his strength.

Once again, she felt like dirt. How had she become so base? She knew then that she had to fight for her faith. She decided she would, come what may. She picked up her Bible and flipped through looking for anything to hang onto until she saw a verse:

> *The things we did in ignorance, God*
> *winked at but now wants all men to*

repent.

She didn't need Kome to tell her what it meant. She went on her knees and repented. She asked God to help her stay true to him this time. She cried until Kome came in. He sat down and gave her an angry look.

"What were you thinking when you let him touch you, Chito? I thought you had stopped this kissing spree?"

She couldn't answer. She had no defence. She knew Simon had told him everything.

"And now you want him to feel guilty when the blood has set him free?" He pushed her head up but she put it down again, holding it with both hands as her tears dropped on the rug. She felt him shake in anger.

"He's a new creature, Chito. Old things are passed away and if God doesn't condemn him, you have no right to."

She knew Kome was right, but she had to blame someone, she just had to blame someone.

"It is so easy for you," she blurted out, "because you don't have these temptations."

He just laughed at her and asked, "Is there any human without temptation? Chito, you have to let God help you, you can't do this on your own."

"How?" she cried, resting her head on his shoulder.

He held her like a baby and said, "Read your Bible, pray every day, just the way we sang it in Sunday school." He pointed out that God wanted to help her if she would let him, as salvation was not a one-off thing but continuous. she knew then that it was time, time to let go and let God.

"Die to Simon", Kome said. "Let him grow, don't be a stumbling block to his faith."

She cried again and he held her, consoling her.

"I feel like being with him all the time," she confessed.

He paused as if in thought. "Stick with God, Chito. Not only can he help you carry your cross, but he can quench that thirst for good, okay?" he concluded as if speaking to a five-year-old.

She nodded in affirmation, beginning a new journey with God. She knew she had to live with her new cravings until God took them away completely. She had to fight, reading her Bible and praying every day so she would have the power to live as his own. But she had learnt a lesson, a bitter one; to love the Lord God above anyone or anything else.

She had given in to Simon and hidden the truth from him because her flesh was being gratified. She had forgotten her first love, the God who had fought countless battles for her. He saved her from rapists but she had poured her gratitude on Simon instead of God. She had seared her heart and looked the other way when the truth came knocking at her door. She had thought she couldn't give Simon up. He, on the other hand, had received Christ and sought purity, giving her up for the love of the God who saved him.

A river of regret flooded her mind, she wished she had fellowshipped with God daily; it would have kept her from falling prey. She wished she had trusted her God-given instincts instead of yielding to deception and letting her flesh rule her. Except the Lord builds a house, they that build, build but in vain.

THE END

GLOSSARY

Abeg: A Pidgin word for 'please.'

Chike: To 'chike' (/chaik/) a girl means to ask her out, pronounced differently from the Igbo name Chike (/cheekay/).

Edikang-Ikong: A Nigerian traditional vegetable soup from Cross River and Akwa Ibom states, made from pumpkin leaves and water leaves (talinum triangulare)

Haba - An exclamation of surprise

Jambitos: or Jambites. The nickname for first-year university students who require the JAMB examinations to get in.

Jo: A Yoruba word normally used to show respect to elders but can also be applied randomly as an exclamation.

Ke: an exclamation of surprise.

Mucheche: Young man

Na: For emphasis

Na: is/ it is *(that na: that is.* **Na so:** *It is so/that is how)* **Na im:** This is it/the thing/the person

No dey: Very fluid Nigerian slang. Can mean 'does not', or 'is not there'.

Ohwo (Owo): A traditional sauce from Edo and Delta states.

Okpari: Nigerian slang for 'it is finished'.

Popsie: Father.

Shack: Versatile Nigerian slang sometimes used to mean intoxication.

AUTHOR'S NOTE

We live in an era where it is more difficult to differentiate between what a Christian should or shouldn't do. There is a lot to drive one away from the cross, but the Bible says that more grace is available to us. Christianity does not make us immune to our humanity. Instead, it acknowledges it and helps us navigate victoriously through life with God's wisdom and grace.

Seeking God and filling ourselves with his word strengthens us because power and might can't do the job. We only prevail by the Spirit of God as we yield to his precepts. Also, self-centredness, offence and bitterness are tools that the enemy uses to keep us away from grace.

Cherish relationships with people who believe and do God's word. In the end, He will be exalted in you. Shalom!

ABOUT THE AUTHOR

Omonefe Oisedebamen Eruotor holds a Bachelor of Arts degree in English and Literature as well as a Master's degree in Development Studies. She loves to read, write, sing, cook and bake; is passionate about the young ones who will become the leaders of tomorrow and writes pieces that can inspire change. To her, every word counts in making the world a better place and creating a healthier tomorrow for the generations following.